# Ruby's STORM

by Amy Hest

pictures by Nancy Cote

Four Winds Press
New York

Maxwell Macmillan Canada   Toronto
Maxwell Macmillan International
New York   Oxford   Singapore   Sydney

For my favorite storm watcher,
Sam

—A.H.

All my love to two great dads
and grandpas—
Edward Marek and Henry Cote
—N.C.

Text copyright © 1994 by Amy Hest
Illustrations copyright © 1994 by Nancy Cote
Four Winds Press
Macmillan Publishing Company
866 Third Avenue
New York, NY 10022
Maxwell Macmillan Canada, Inc.
1200 Eglinton Avenue East
Suite 200
Don Mills, Ontario M3C 3N1
Macmillan Publishing Company is part of the
Maxwell Communication Group of Companies.
First edition
Printed and bound in Singapore

10 9 8 7 6 5 4 3 2 1

The text of this book is set in Antique Olive.
The illustrations are rendered in gouache.
Book design by Christy Hale

Library of Congress Cataloging-in-Publication Data
Hest, Amy.
Ruby's storm / by Amy Hest ; pictures by Nancy Cote.—1st ed.
p.   cm.
Summary: On a stormy spring day, Ruby makes her way through the
city to visit her grandfather.
ISBN 0-02-743160-6
[1. Storms—Fiction.   2. Grandfathers—Fiction.   3. City and town
life—Fiction.]   I. Cote, Nancy, ill.   II. Title.
PZ7.H4375Ru  1994
[E]—dc20
92-31242

**R**uby lined her basket with a cherry-colored napkin.

She packed up seven cookies and a leftover brownie. She packed two china cups, crunching paper between them so they wouldn't get cracked.

After that she packed a fat green candle in a candle holder, her checkerboard and checkers, and a special pad for keeping score. (Ruby liked to keep score.)

She slid her poncho off the hook in the closet, then slipped it over her head. This poncho was brand-new, with a big yellow pocket in front and a yellow hood, too. Her boots were last year's boots, but they had a fine, fuzzy lining and a star buckle at each ankle.

"I am ready." Ruby hugged Mama, hard, around the waist.

"Brave Ruby." Mama hugged, too.

They took turns blowing kisses all the time Ruby was running down the winding stairs.

Clouds rolled over tall buildings, traveling faster than trucks. They pitched and dipped and bounced along. They blew and bucked, then bumped the sun right out of the sky.

Spring storm.
The city looked like night, and Ruby
shivered.

Umbrellas shot up and windows shot down. Awnings flapped, coats flapped, a lady chased her hat. "Come back!" she cried. "Come back, hat!"

Ruby's poncho blew up and up, and she laughed out loud, dancing off the stoop.

The wind pushed at her face, but Ruby pushed back.

"Hold on, Grampa! Brave Ruby is coming!"
Rain pelted her nose and it was ice-cold,
but it tickled, too. Ruby ran, but not too fast.
She was fighting the wind and the cold and
the dark.

She was running and pushing and wishing, wishing she had a dog called Romeo. Big Romeo would bark his loud bark and the wind would quiver and quake. Then Ruby and Romeo would skip right on to Grampa's house. They would hop in all the puddles.

Ruby shivered and pushed the wind.

At 85th Street the greengrocer chased apples and pears.

Across 86th Street the newsman held down his papers.

5th
treet
ruit
stand

86th

On the corner of 87th the lady who made pizza pulled down her shade.

At 88th Street, Grampa's street, Ruby's hood slid off. She felt like a girl who was standing in a poncho in the shower.

Grampa's house was over the bakery, and
it always smelled like warm toast inside.

Grampa rubbed Ruby's hair with a towel.

The table was small and round and all set
up with two place mats facing the window
and the storm. Grampa's napkins were
cherry-colored. The teapot was silver, but
there was hot chocolate inside.

Ruby arranged cookies and the
brownie on a platter.

She unpacked the china cups,
and not one thing got cracked.

Grampa lit the candle in
the candle holder.

Ruby and Grampa ate all the cookies, and then they shared the brownie.

They took turns pouring hot chocolate until there was nothing left to pour.

Afterward they played checkers. Grampa
won, but Ruby got to keep score.